FUTUREKIND

THE GENESIS

ANGEL GHOSH

To the ones who have always felt different,
who see beyond the veil of what is and sense what could
be—
This is for you.

For those who question reality,
who believe pain births clarity,
and who choose truth over comfort—
You are not alone.

And to the quiet souls guiding us from beyond the
boundaries of time,
Thank you for the whispers.

Contents

Contents

Foreword

There comes a moment in every life when the familiar cracks—revealing something deeper beneath the surface of what we call reality.

This book was born from that crack.

Futurekind: Genesis is not just a story. It is a question disguised as fiction, built on real threads—science, ancient knowledge, and the strange synchronicities that bind our world. As the pages unfold, you will walk the edge of known truth and speculative wonder, where reason and revelation meet.

You may feel a sense of déjà vu. That's intentional.

Because some stories are not invented.
They are remembered.

And some journeys don't begin with a step...
They begin with a feeling you've been here before.

If you've found this book, it means the time has come to remember.

— Angel Ghosh

Preface

This is not a story about the end of the world.
It is a story about what comes after we stop pretending.

Futurekind: Genesis was born from silence—from the space between thoughts, where something ancient still speaks. I did not write this book to entertain. I wrote it to awaken.

In a time when humanity is louder than ever yet more disconnected than ever before, I began to see the threads—the codes hidden in biology, the echoes of our past buried beneath ice, the quiet knowing inside each of us that we are not what we've been told. Through Orakai's eyes, I revisited those questions:

Who are we, really?

Why do we feel so far from home?

And what if the next phase of human evolution isn't physical, but conscious?

This is the beginning of that question.
The genesis of a future no longer bound by fear, identity, or time.

If you feel something stir as you read, that's not by accident.
The signal has reached you.

Welcome to the story behind all stories.
Welcome to Futurekind.

— Angel Ghosh

Acknowledgements

This book is the culmination of years of observation, questioning, and the courage to walk paths that often made no sense until they did.

To my sister—your presence, wisdom, and quiet strength echo through every word on these pages. You have always seen what others overlook. Thank you for believing in me when I questioned everything, including myself.

To those who have walked in and out of my life—you were all chapters in my becoming. Some tested me, others taught me. All transformed me.

To the thinkers, seekers, and quiet rebels who feel the world a little differently—this story was written for you. May it awaken what has long been sleeping inside.

And lastly, to the unknown intelligence that weaves life's silent patterns—thank you for the signs, the signals, and the timing. I only hope I've listened well enough.

— Angel Ghosh

Prologue

What if everything you believed about life, evolution, and history... was just the surface layer?

Orakai never fit in — not because she didn't try, but because something deeper always called her.

When a quiet voice stirs her consciousness and a long-forgotten memory rises within her, she's pulled into a web of hidden patterns, ancient symbols, and truths buried beneath both science and myth.

From the genetic code we all share to the frozen secrets beneath Antarctica, Futurekind: Genesis unravels a forgotten legacy encoded in our very DNA.

This is not just a story of awakening. It's a reckoning — with the past, with the system, and with the very fabric of what we call reality.

For readers of minimalist sci-fi, spiritual thrillers, and seekers of hidden knowledge.

The Genesis was only the spark. The flame is coming.

CHAPTER ONE

THE ONE CELL

Before time had memory, before the continents rose, before the word "life" had meaning—there was LUCA.

The *Last Universal Common Ancestor* which existed over 3.5 billion years ago in a world vastly different from ours. LUCA was not the first living thing, but it was the organism from which all known life on Earth descended.

Bacteria, archaea, and eukaryotes—every blade of grass, every living cell in the human body, every fungus under ancient forest floors—can trace their molecular lineage back to this single root. Unlike the hypothetical primitive forms that may have preceded it, LUCA was already remarkably complex. Genetic reconstruction suggests LUCA possessed a genome of around 355 genes—coding for proteins responsible for essential functions like energy metabolism, cell membrane structure, and the translation of RNA to proteins.

It likely relied on ribozymes and metal-rich cofactors to facilitate biochemical reactions. Even today, many of LUCA's genetic signatures are preserved in the deepest branches of the tree of life.

LUCA did not live on the Earth's surface. The surface was inhospitable, bombarded by solar radiation and lacking a protective ozone layer. Instead, LUCA found refuge in the darkness of the deep ocean—specifically near hydrothermal vents known as black smokers.

These vents expelled mineral-laden water, creating strong chemical gradients that allowed the first metabolic pathways to form. Here, in the shadows of the Earth's crust, molecules organized into mechanisms, and mechanisms into life.

Modern research paints LUCA not as a solitary microbe but as part of a communal gene-sharing population. Horizontal gene transfer was rampant, allowing life to experiment, borrow, and adapt rapidly.

This genetic exchange created the foundation for evolution and diversity. LUCA was not a single spark—it was a network of sparks, lighting the fire of biology.

Despite the vast time that separates us from LUCA, pieces of its legacy are still encoded in us.

The same genetic letters. The same protein-building tools. The same spark of self-replication. Our cells are built on LUCA's blueprint, and every breath we take is a quiet tribute to that primordial ancestor.

And it goes further than just humans. Birds, snakes, whales, trees, mushrooms—all life shares the same fundamental genetic code. The sequences may differ, but the language is the same.

The four-letter code—A, T, C, and G—is universal. The proteins that help us digest, grow, and repair exist in similar forms in vastly different species. This commonality is not symbolic—it is literal.

A crow on a branch, a serpent in the sand, a sunflower bending toward light—all of them are distant relatives. They are echoes of LUCA, just as we are.

This is not poetic. It is molecular truth. And yet, despite this profound connection, humanity often forgets. We treat nature as separate, lesser, expendable. But in doing so, we betray our own ancestry.

We deny the bond that ties every creature, every leaf, every drop of blood to the very first cell that dared to divide.

To know LUCA is to understand that we are not alone—we never were. We are family, spread across kingdoms, continents, and forms. And if we truly grasp that truth, perhaps we will begin to treat the Earth not as a possession, but as a shared inheritance. But the mystery runs deeper.

LUCA's complexity suggests it emerged from even earlier prebiotic systems—perhaps protocells composed of simple lipid membranes and RNA-like molecules. These systems may have formed in mineral pores, shielded from the chaos above.

There, life may have tested its early chemistry, slowly converging toward stability, efficiency, and self-sustainability.

This process remains one of science's greatest puzzles. How did non-living matter make the leap into life? Why did certain molecules combine in precisely the right way to build something that could copy itself, harvest energy, and adapt to change?

Scientists speak of natural selection, chemical inevitability, and environmental pressure. But even with these tools, the birth of life feels like a miracle of improbability.

Was it pure chance? A confluence of favorable conditions? Or something embedded in the structure of the universe—a kind of biological inevitability?

LUCA is the threshold, the moment when matter gained memory, when chemistry took its first breath. Everything that followed—plants, animals, language, consciousness—was encoded in that breath.

The implications stretch beyond biology. If LUCA arose here, in Earth's oceans, under specific yet replicable conditions, could it happen elsewhere? Are there other worlds where LUCA's cousins began similar stories—silent, cellular whispers waiting to be heard?

We have decoded parts of LUCA's genome. We have recreated its proteins in labs. But LUCA's purpose, if any, remains unknown. It may have been an accident, a consequence of entropy and time. Or it may be the echo of something deeper—a principle woven into the fabric of reality itself.

Science can describe how life works. How nucleotides pair. How ribosomes read. But the "why"—the purpose, if any—remains untouched. LUCA reminds us that we are not just flesh and thought, but heritage—stretching back through eons to a single, fragile beginning.

LUCA began the story. But it did not end there.

Beneath our skin, in every cell, LUCA still whispers. And some, unknowingly, begin to listen.

CHAPTER TWO

THE AWAKENING OF ORAKAI

It happened one evening. No relics. No strange lights.

Just the silence of her small room, her journal open, half a sentence written, then—

Stillness.

A pause in her breath. A flicker in her spine.

Like the universe leaned in, gently.

A thought—not hers—whispered across her mind like wind brushing old stone.

"They told you to believe without questioning."

She blinked. Sat still.

The sentence came again, clearer this time—like it had always been there, waiting.

"You thought it was obedience.

You thought it was faith.

It was a technology."

She didn't understand why, but tears gathered quietly in her eyes. Not from sadness—something clse. Something like... remembering.

"Belief is the key, Orakai.

Not to control the world—but to choose which one you live in."

She looked down at her trembling hands.

Nothing around her had changed. The walls. The flickering lamp. The quiet hum of night outside.

But inside—everything shifted.

The old stories. The gods. The rules of what was possible...

"They weren't gods," the voice whispered, now within her. "They were mirrors.

You were always the architect."

Orakai didn't speak. She just sat with it.

No questions. No fear.

Only this quiet knowing:

Something ancient had just been unlocked in her.

And nothing would be the same again.

That night, she lay down without closing her journal.

The lamp still flickered gently beside her bed.

She fell asleep with a softness she hadn't known in years.

In her dream, she rose.

Not from her bed—but from her form.

Weightless, lucid. More aware than she'd ever been while awake.

Around her stretched a vast, glowing plain.

No ground. No sky. Just light and silence and something... vast.

And then—herself.

But not quite.

A version of her standing calmly in the distance, radiant and ageless, eyes like deep time.

Orakai walked toward her, barefoot on nothing.

"Who are you?" she whispered.

The being smiled.

"You. But without fear.

You. From the timeline where you remembered first."

Orakai's heart beat faster.

"Is this a dream?"

The answer came not in words—but as a knowing:

"This is not a dream.

This is where dreams come from."

And in that place, belief wasn't a question.

It was the air.

The gravity.

The code.

She woke before dawn, breath steady, heart calm.

She didn't remember everything.

But one thing was clear.

She was not just Orakai anymore.

Something higher had seen her.

And she had seen it back.

It was a quiet morning when Orakai first felt it again—the shift. A subtle hum in her awareness, a whisper that curled into her thoughts like the scent of smoke before a fire.

It wasn't just a dream—it was an awakening. And it wouldn't let her go.

She sat in the same room, her walls lined with books and scattered notes. Her journal still lay open from the night before.

The sentence she'd never finished seemed almost irrelevant now. A doorway had opened, and she couldn't unsee what was on the other side.

Orakai had always been different.

While others were drawn to the noise of life, she gravitated toward its quiet echoes. As a child, she'd sat in the back of classrooms, listening more to what wasn't said than what was. She hadn't just learned—she'd absorbed. Interpreted. Connected.

Her apartment was a shrine to curiosity: worn notebooks, diagrams, stacks of books about ancient civilizations, metaphysics, coded languages, and theories others dismissed as fringe. But to her, they were pieces. Fragments of something whole.

And now, at 22, the picture was becoming clear.

Everything in her life—every encounter, every dream, every strange coincidence—had been part of something deliberate. A kind of design. And she wasn't just an observer anymore. She was part of the code.

She remembered what her fifth-grade teacher, Mr. Larson, once told her: "Don't just memorize. Understand. Find the connections." At the time, it had felt like generic advice. But now, it echoed like prophecy.

The strange insights she used to brush off, the unexplainable intuition—none of it was random. She had always been decoding something, long before she knew it was there.

And Miko. Her sister had always known. Not explicitly, not in words, but in the way she saw Orakai. Miko had never questioned her strangeness. She accepted it. Nourished it.

Their late-night conversations about fate, coincidence, and meaning weren't just bonding moments—they were transmissions. Orakai now saw how those conversations had shaped her path. Miko was part of the pattern too.

Everything mattered.

The grief.

The isolation.

The books she clung to when the world made no sense.

The feeling that life was more than it appeared.

Now, it all pulsed beneath her skin like a second heartbeat.

She stood up, walked to the window. The city moved beneath her like clockwork—fast, noisy, oblivious. But Orakai saw the hidden gears turning beneath it all.

The world wasn't random.

It was encrypted.

And belief... was the cipher.

Her phone buzzed, breaking the silence. A message from Miko.

"Are you okay? You've been quiet today. I'm making us some tea. Let's talk."

Orakai smiled, her eyes still shimmering with the echo of the dream.

She knew the next step.

She didn't have to carry it alone.

Not anymore.

She picked up her journal and finally finished the sentence.

"It was never about finding the truth."

"It was about remembering it."

The Pattern Beneath the Noise

The morning sun spilled through the curtains as Orakai stirred awake, still haunted by her dreams. They weren't nightmares. More like fragments of memories—or visions—from somewhere ancient. Spirals made of stardust. Birds with eyes like galaxies. Snakes made of lightning. And through it all, a calm, persistent voice whispered, "Everything speaks. Listen."

The whisper had trailed her from sleep into waking, a murmur lingering just beneath consciousness.

For the first time in years, her mind felt startlingly clear—so sharp it almost hurt. She sat at her cluttered desk, pushing aside cold coffee cups, crumpled cigarette packs, and notebooks filled with scribbled margins and half-formed thoughts.

A single word surfaced from the noise: LUCA—Last Universal Common Ancestor. Mr. Smith in science class had mentioned it once, almost offhandedly, as if it were just another bullet point on a syllabus.

But now, the weight of it pressed into her. The origin of everything. She stared at her laptop as it blinked patiently. Something had shifted. She opened a new tab.

"What is LUCA?"

Before the browser could finish loading, she opened another window—ChatGPT.

She typed:

"Tell me everything about LUCA – the Last Universal Common Ancestor."

As she read through the AI's response, a quiet awe settled in her chest. LUCA wasn't just a theory. It was the origin.

The most ancient ancestor of every living organism on Earth. Not a fully formed being, but a communal network of early life—cells in the boiling oceans of primordial Earth, around 4 billion years ago.

It wasn't male or female. It wasn't even conscious. But it carried the building blocks of everything that would come after.

Birds. Plants. Snakes. Humans

All encoded with the same ancestral software.

She whispered to herself, "We're cousins. All of us."

That simple truth hit her like lightning.

She opened another chat window.

"Do birds and humans share DNA?"

"Yes," ChatGPT responded, "Birds and humans share many genes. The genetic code is universal across almost all life on Earth."

That was the part no one seemed to grasp: The genetic code was shared. Not similar. Shared. The same four-letter alphabet—A, T, G, C—woven in different arrangements to build all of life.

It felt holy. Every bird, every plant, every human being carried LUCA's ancient whispers in their DNA.

A spiral code passed down through eons. She whispered to herself, "We are all just different expressions of the same original story."

Her eyes welled up with a strange mixture of awe and sadness. How had humanity missed this? Why were we so divided—by race, by nation, by belief—when we were literally relatives?

She thought back to biology class. Her teacher, Ms. Rina, had once said, "The human genome is 99.9% identical among all people. And even more shockingly—we share about 60% of our DNA with bananas. Life is not a hierarchy; it's a web."

At the time, the class had laughed. Orakai hadn't.

She had felt it. And now it clicked.

There were recurring symbols in all she read: spirals, symmetry, code, repetition, reflection. Whether it was DNA, galaxies, or mythologies from across the world—they all pointed to patterns that repeated across scales, from the micro to the cosmic.

She jotted into her notebook:

"Fractals of life. LUCA. All is pattern. All is kin."

CHAPTER FOUR

THE GREAT CURIOSITY

Her phone buzzed. A message from Miko:

"Hey O, I've been thinking about our talk the other day. You still awake in your 'science den'? Wanna call later?"

Miko lived two cities away now. They hadn't seen each other in months. But Miko always sensed when something big was stirring in Orakai's world.

Orakai replied:

"Yes. I found something. It's... massive."

Later that evening, they video called. Miko sat by her window, sunlight falling in her room, sipping tea. Orakai, surrounded by paper, notebooks, and glowing tabs, looked like she hadn't slept.

"Let me guess," Miko smiled. "You fell down another rabbit hole."

Orakai nodded, breathless. "But this one's different. It's not just another theory or fact. It's the connection. LUCA. The genetic unity. All life.

I asked ChatGPT, and it confirmed what I've always felt but couldn't prove. We're all stitched together. Everything. From ferns to falcons. From us... to mushrooms."

Miko leaned in. "You mean like... actual shared code?"

"Yes," Orakai said. "It's not metaphorical. It's biological. The same coding language. Like the universe left us a signature."

There was silence for a moment.

Then Miko said, "So if everything is made from the same alphabet, then maybe consciousness isn't just in us. Maybe it's in everything. Just tuned to different frequencies."

Orakai's eyes lit up. "Exactly. That's what I'm feeling. Like life is one giant organism that's forgotten it's whole."

That night, Orakai pulled out her journal and began mapping the patterns: LUCA at the center. Branches spiraling outward like a tree. Fungi, animals, humans, flowers, whales. She drew connecting lines—scientific facts paired with ancient myths. The Tree of Life. Serpent symbolism. Spiral galaxies. DNA helices.

She opened her Journal and wrote at the top:

"Everything alive carries the memory of LUCA. And the pattern is still speaking—through our cells, our stories, and our questions."

It was all connected. The science. The symbols. The intuition. And now, with tools like ChatGPT, she wasn't just guessing anymore. She was researching with intention, cross-checking with logic, merging the mystical with the measurable.

A single thought echoed in her mind as she stared at her notes:

"This is not new knowledge. It's ancient remembrance."

And with that, she turned the page...

CHAPTER FIVE

TEMPORARY ATTACHMENTS

Orakai met Riko when she least expected to—at a time in her life when everything was shifting beneath the surface. She wasn't looking for anyone. She was deep in thought, unraveling the layers of life, nature, and consciousness. Her days were filled with research and reflection.

Riko entered quietly, like a breeze slipping through a half-open window.

They crossed paths through mutual friends at a small gathering—nothing unusual, nothing forced.

He had an ease to him, an honesty in how he spoke and listened. Conversations started off light—shared movie list, sharing reels, silly jokes. But somewhere between those casual talks, a deeper current formed.

She didn't plan to fall in love. In fact, she had grown to believe love might just be another story society built too tightly around people.

But something about Riko made her soften.

Maybe it was the way he, too, seemed detached from the usual chase of life.

Maybe it was his calm, his presence, his way of simply being there.

Orakai, who had grown used to standing alone with her thoughts, found herself wanting just him. Just this quiet, grounding connection.

For a while, it felt simple. But life had other plans.

What they had wasn't built for permanence.

It was real, yes. But temporary—two souls walking together through a shared chapter, not an entire book.

There were fights and bitterness at a point. Just different paths slowly becoming clearer. Responsibilities, unspoken needs, timing, distance—so many small things quietly adding up to one truth:

They loved each other, but not for a lifetime. They were meant to be there for each other, not with each other.

The ending came like a soft rain—no thunder, no storm. Just a knowing.

They moved on.

Orakai grieved in her own way, not through tears, but through thought. Through silence. Through understanding.

In her Journal She wrote:

"Maybe some people come into our lives not to stay,

but to remind us of what we are capable of feeling.

Maybe love isn't always about forever.

Maybe it's about awakening something we had forgotten."

She didn't regret any of it.

Riko taught her something more valuable than comfort—he showed her that even in a temporary moment, there could be depth, realness, and transformation.

And that life—this constantly flowing, ever-evolving thing—was larger than attachment.

The purpose was always higher.

Not relationships. Not security.

But learning. Remembering. Living with awareness.

As Orakai continued walking her path, she carried Riko in memory, not in longing.

Life was the highest.

Love was beautiful, but not the goal.

The goal was **clarity**...

CHAPTER SIX

THE INHERITANCE OF STARS

The days that followed were quieter.

Not lonely—just quieter.

Riko's absence didn't echo through Orakai's life like a void, but like space being made for something else. She filled it with walks, silence, curiosity, and long evenings of asking questions she never had time to before.

It was in those still spaces that something else began to awaken.

She started noticing patterns again—only this time, deeper. Not just in thoughts or coincidences, but in genetics, geometry, stories, and symbols.

She remembered something from school—a faint line in a textbook—about how all living organisms, from birds to trees to snakes, share the same fundamental genetic code.

That stuck with her.

"If every living thing is built from the same letters," she wrote in her notebook,

"Then we're not separate species. We're one long sentence... spoken by the Earth."

The idea gripped her more than any love ever had.

Late at night, she'd sit cross-legged with a blanket, coffee and a cigarette, and search terms typed into her browser like:

"Human DNA and stardust."

"Symmetry in plants and ancient architecture."

"Are our cells remembering something we forgot?"

Sometimes she asked ChatGPT, but not always. She had learned that not every answer needed a source. Some things had to arrive.

She revisited old knowledge with fresh eyes:

How over 90% of human DNA is considered "non-coding," often called junk DNA, yet it carries evolutionary memory.

How sacred geometry appears in plants and galaxies alike.

How ancient civilizations knew things modern science is only now rediscovering.

It made her wonder: What else do we carry inside us?

What if there's something encoded—not just biologically, but energetically?

Orakai started journaling every morning, writing not about her feelings, but what she noticed—the alignment of things, the echoes of patterns, the subtle threads that felt too consistent to be random.

"Maybe our ancestors weren't telling stories, "She thought one day.

"Maybe they were trying to pass on memory."

She paused and stared out her window.

The sky looked different. Not just beautiful—intentional. She began to sense that the journey wasn't just about understanding life. It was about remembering something ancient that life itself was trying to express through her.

Not aliens.

Not magic.

Not prophecy.

But inheritance.

An inheritance not of money or land—but of knowledge. A kind passed on not by family, but by existence.

You are not separate from this.

You are it.

And it's remembering itself through you.

And suddenly, everything around her—the noise, the rush, the endless chase for jobs, homes, status, marriage, love—felt like distractions.

Beautiful, yes. But not the point.

"Life isn't about owning," she wrote.

"It's about awakening."

The world had normalized a strange blindness: chasing things that fade while ignoring the truth that was staring us in the face. The stars had always been speaking. The Earth had always been teaching. The DNA had always been whispering:

"There is something more."

Orakai didn't know what she would become, or what her exact mission was—but she knew one thing:

She would no longer look away!

CHAPTER SEVEN

THE PULSE OF THE EARTH

It started with a hum.

Not a sound, exactly. More like a frequency.

It came to Orakai when she walked barefoot in the garden one morning. The dew on the grass. The cold, uneven touch of the soil beneath her. The wind brushing against her arms like an invisible hand.

And then... the stillness.

But not empty stillness—aware stillness. Like something ancient had noticed her.

She froze.

The world wasn't just background noise anymore. It felt alive. Observant. Connected. Like the trees were more than trees, the birds more than birds, the air more than just oxygen.

"It's been here all along," she whispered, standing in the silence.

"And I've been too loud to hear it."

Orakai began spending more time in nature—not as a visitor, but as a part of it. She watched the clouds move with meaning. She followed the spiral patterns in ferns, in seashells, in galaxies. She listened—not with her ears, but with something deeper.

There was a rhythm beneath it all. A slow, patient pulse.

The ancients had known it. The Vedas called it Prana. The Chinese called it Qi. Modern physics might call it zero-point energy or background vibration. But Orakai didn't need a term. She could feel it.

The Earth was not a dead rock.

It was a sentient organism.

And we were the cells in its body.

She remembered something she heard in a podcast:

"If humans are sick, it's because the Earth is sick. And maybe we're the fever trying to heal her—or the virus making it worse."

That idea echoed in her chest for days.

She started meditating, not just to calm herself, but to tune in. She realized that thoughts weren't just hers—they were part of a much larger web. Some were echoes. Some were signals. Some were invitations.

She didn't talk about this with many people. It was too strange. Too still. The world was always moving—scrolling, shouting, consuming. But this... this was different.

One afternoon, sitting on the porch, she saw a neighborhood dog come trotting by. Its eyes met hers, and something stirred inside her—a deep, almost ancient recognition.

It wasn't the first time. Dogs had always made her feel something she couldn't explain. A presence. A soul. A silent understanding, like they knew something we didn't. As a child, she always felt safer when one was around. Now, with everything she was exploring, that feeling returned—but with new questions.

So, she searched:

"Why do dogs and humans have such a strong bond?"

"How long have dogs been with us?"

"Can dogs sense human emotions and energy?"

And what she found astonished her.

Dogs have been with humans for over 15,000 years—the first animals to be domesticated.

They evolved alongside us, not just physically, but emotionally. Their brains light up when they see human faces. They can detect illness, stress, seizures, and even death—not just through smell, but something that felt like intuition.

Some researchers even suggested dogs were key to early human survival. They protected, guided, and healed.

"They weren't just pets," she whispered.

"They were messengers."

Orakai felt chills.

Maybe dogs weren't just man's best friend. Maybe they were guardians—bridge-beings between instinct and love, nature and humanity. Maybe they were one of the last living examples of what unconditional presence looked like.

She watched that same dog curl up in the sunlight near a tree. Peaceful. Aware. Aligned.

"They've always remembered," she thought.

"Even when we forgot."

In that moment, she understood something quietly profound:

The Earth speaks not only through stars and storms, but through animals. Through loyalty. Through instinct. Through the soft eyes of a creature that has no agenda—just being.

Orakai continued writing in her journal:

"There is a heartbeat beneath the noise.

The Earth is not waiting for us to save it.

It's waiting for us to remember we're part of it."

The disconnection—between humans and nature, between humans and themselves—was not an accident. It was the root of all suffering.

And the path forward wasn't about saving the planet. It was about coming home to it.

CHAPTER EIGHT

THE MEMORY OF FIRE

Orakai sat in her room with her journal, a warm cup of black coffee, and a mind full of fragments. Not broken pieces, but ancient echoes, connecting like constellations across time.

She didn't believe in coincidences anymore.

Not when so many civilizations—separated by oceans and languages—had left behind the same fingerprints.

Pyramids. Flood myths. Sky gods. Fallen knowledge.

And always... fire.

But as she kept digging, something even more shocking emerged—the rise of religions.

She hadn't planned to go there. Religion was sensitive, sacred for many. But truth didn't care for comfort.

What she found was deeply unsettling. And yet, it made everything make sense.

The Fire Was Caged

At first, spirituality was natural.

Human beings observed nature. The sun gave life. The moon influenced tides. Trees healed. The stars told stories. There was reverence, not fear.

But then, stories became structures.

Symbols became systems.

And power stepped in.

Religions began rising—not as reflections of truth, but as tools. Tools to control, to divide, to dictate.

The divine became external. Holiness became hierarchy.

And slowly, the sacred fire of inner connection... was caged.

"They turned personal awakening into organized belief," Orakai noted.

"And then punished anyone who questioned it."

It was a massive realization.

Most people had outsourced their souls.

Instead of looking within, they memorized verses.

Instead of asking why, they repeated Because...

Instead of becoming light, they worshipped it from a distance.

And behind all of it—institutions.

Kings. Priests. Empires. Governments.

They weren't all evil. But they were afraid.

Afraid of a human being who could think.

Who could feel.

Who could see the whole picture.

Orakai began to notice something more disturbing:

Religions didn't always preserve ancient truths—they often distorted them.

"The stories of the legends," she wrote,

"Weren't meant to be worshipped. They were meant to be understood."

She saw it clearly now: the "gods" of myth were perhaps ancient humans—or something more.

Wise, evolved, maybe even extraterrestrial. But humans turned them into deities, separated from themselves.

It became holy to believe.

And dangerous to ask. And through that fear, manipulation grew.

Orakai went deeper.

She started reading declassified documents.

Listening to whistleblowers.

Watching old press conferences that had long been buried under clickbait and noise.

There were patterns.

UFO sightings covered up.

Technologies buried.

Archaeological discoveries in Antarctica, the Middle East, even under the oceans—vanishing into silence.

And always, the same message from those who spoke out:

"They don't want us to know."

Who were they?

Not some cartoonish villain behind a curtain. But a system—layers of governments, corporations, defense programs, religious bodies—all with one common interest:

Control.

Because true freedom, true knowledge, is dangerous to the world they've built.

"If we knew who we really are," Orakai wrote,

"We wouldn't need governments. We wouldn't need permission to live."

And maybe that was the fear.

Not that humans were weak.

But that humans were powerful.

And that power, awakened, would end every fake structure built on lies.

But things were changing.

More people were asking questions.

More truths were surfacing.

More souls were awakening—not through violence, but through clarity.

The fire was returning.

Not to destroy. But to illuminate.

And Orakai knew this was just the beginning.

"We don't need a new religion," she whispered.

"We need a new remembrance."

She looked at the candle beside her and smiled.

The flame flickered gently.

Wild. Alive. Free.

CHAPTER NINE

THE ARCHITECTS

Orakai couldn't sleep. Not from restlessness, but from revelation.

The symbols she once overlooked in ancient carvings, the architectural wonders that had stood for millennia, the myths that had survived destruction—all of it began to point to one question:

Who built this... and why?

She wasn't talking about simple structures.

She meant the impossible ones.

The Pyramids of Giza, aligned perfectly with Orion's Belt.

Machu Picchu, at high altitudes with water channels more precise than modern engineering. Stonehenge, Teotihuacan, Ba'albek, Easter Island, and Derinkuyu—the underground city deep beneath Turkey.

"If we think cavemen built this with ropes and rocks... we're insulting their genius—or ignoring someone else's."

She started calling them The Architects.

Not necessarily aliens.

Not necessarily humans.

But something—or someone—who understood frequency, geometry, astronomy, and the human mind far beyond our current comprehension.

These structures weren't just homes or temples.

They were maps.

Antennas.

Messages left in stone.

She ran simulations, watched documentaries and read articles—but still used it for leads. One article led to another. One photo from a drone would reveal a previously hidden alignment. One book would hint that even the Nazca lines were visible only from the sky for a reason.

She wrote in her journal:

"It's not that we're alone. It's that we've forgotten who walked with us."

Maybe these Architects were once revered as gods.

Maybe they were just evolved humans from a previous cycle.

Or maybe they came from elsewhere—but not for conquest... for contribution.

They encoded knowledge in temples, in legends, in the design of the human body itself.

Every structure mirrored the stars, the human brain or the ratio of life. There was intelligence embedded in everything.

But why hide it?

Because not everyone was ready.

Knowledge without wisdom becomes power. And power corrupts.

So, the Architects left their messages—only visible to the ones willing to see.

Orakai sat back, her mind alive.

"They weren't just building. They were remembering. They were telling us—we are more. We always were."

She circled one phrase over and over in her notebook:

"We are the descendants of the Architects. The legacy is in our DNA."

She looked up at the sky that night—not to pray, not to plead—but to connect.

Because now she knew: Humanity was never abandoned. We just stopped listening.

CHAPTER TEN

THE AWAKENING CODE

Orakai wasn't chasing spirituality or religion anymore. She was chasing the truth—quietly, logically, and alone.

In her room, scattered with notes and her cold cup of coffee, she kept returning to one core idea:

"We are more than we think, and less than we pretend."

She had read about the junk DNA—the 98% of the human genome that didn't code for proteins. Scientists named it useless, but many were beginning to question that label.

Was it really "junk"? Or just un-decoded?

Maybe it held instructions not for how we're built—but for how we think, feel, evolve.

Unfinished Design

Patterns existed everywhere.

The spirals in galaxies. The symmetry of snowflakes. The branching of neurons and trees—almost identical.

Orakai wrote in her journal:

"The same geometry runs through leaves, lungs, and lightning. So, who's to say we're not running on a system that was built once—and echoed forever?"

She didn't need myths anymore.

The math was enough.

She started simplifying her life—less clutter, fewer screens, more observation.

She noticed how her memory sharpened when she read physical books. How silence helped her understand things she couldn't explain. How certain thoughts came not from "thinking" but from simply noticing.

She wasn't becoming spiritual; she was becoming aware.

"Maybe consciousness isn't about reaching higher," she thought,

"It's about being more precise."

Like tuning an instrument—she wasn't trying to play new music, just hear what was already playing more clearly.

Orakai still used the internet. Still talked to Miko. Still watched the news sometimes. But her filters had changed.

She stopped reacting.

She started noticing more of what wasn't said.

She understood silence better than noise.

"We've been looking for signs in the sky," she wrote. "But the real signs are in our cells."

She began seeing herself not as "one human in a broken world,"

but as one part of a working mechanism—a life form designed by time, memory, and nature.

And that changed everything.

Later that week, Orakai went for a walk. No headphones. Just the world.

She passed a street dog—old, with a limp, resting under a tea stall.

The man tossed it a biscuit, without a word. The dog wagged its tail once.

That moment stayed with her.

"Even he knows. We're all connected. No theory needed."

It wasn't about empathy. It was about awareness.

She recalled how, as a child, she always felt things others didn't.

The silent fear in a teacher's voice.

The way her sister, Miko, would smile when she was actually sad.

The quiet in the air before bad news.

It was never mystical.

It was just observation.

Back home, she wrote something bold:

"We're not separate from nature. We are nature.

The only species arrogant enough to think otherwise."

Her curiosity was no longer about "why the world was broken."

She knew the answer.

It was because most people didn't understand this one truth:

That evolution wasn't just a scientific process.

It was a test of humility.

To realize how small we are.

And yet, how connected we are to everything.

That night, she sat with her sister Miko on a video call. They laughed about old memories, shared silence, and spoke about life as if it were an unfinished story.

"You know," Orakai said, "maybe the real awakening isn't some big event. Maybe it's just... remembering that we're part of something older, and much bigger than us."

"The greatest enemy of knowledge is not ignorance, it is the illusion of knowledge."

- Stephen Hawking

CHAPTER ELEVEN

THE FORBIDDEN LAYER

The more Orakai explored, the more she realized—this wasn't just about science.

It wasn't just about consciousness either.

This was about buried truths—literally.

What Was Hidden Was Always There

She came across an image one night—Göbekli Tepe.

An ancient structure far older than the Egyptian pyramids.

Carved with symbols no one could decode.

"Why did they bury it?" she wondered.

Most ancient ruins are eroded by time.

But this one was intentionally hidden—as if someone didn't want it found.

The more she looked, the more places she found:

The Great Pyramids of Giza—built with astronomical precision.

Puma Punku in Bolivia—machine-like stone cuts in an age with no known tools.

The ancient city of Mohenjo Daro—where bodies were found as if suddenly destroyed, with radiation levels higher than expected.

Orakai started asking a dangerous question:

"Are we really the most advanced humans that ever existed?"

Then Realized, History is Filtered

Most schoolbooks taught the same arc: cavemen → farmers → kings → scientists → us.

But there were gaps. Too many unexplained jumps in technology. Too many stories of fire from the sky, gods descending, civilizations vanishing overnight.

She wrote:

"If even 10% of these stories are real—our entire understanding of human history is a lie of omission."

Myths are Manuals, the legends suddenly felt different.

Prometheus bringing fire.

The Sumerian Anunnaki.

The Hindu Vimanas flying through the sky.

The Egyptian "Djed" pillars—once thought symbolic, now resembling energy devices.

"What if these weren't myths?" she asked.

"What if they were manuals—coded in symbols, passed as stories?"

Orakai also stumbled on cases of scientists whose work vanished:

Wilhelm Reich, who studied orgone energy, arrested and erased. Nikola Tesla's work on free wireless energy, confiscated. Researchers into human biofields, mocked until defunded.

"Truth doesn't disappear because it's false," she noted.

"It disappears because it's dangerous."

The Forbidden Layer is Everywhere

It wasn't just in archives.

It was in the ruins.

It was in our DNA.

It was in the questions we're told not to ask.

Orakai didn't believe in fantasy.

She believed in patterns.

And the deeper she went, the clearer the pattern became:

We are a species with amnesia. And someone benefits from keeping it that way.

She no longer waited for proof.

She followed the silence. Because what's not talked about is often what matters the most.

CHAPTER TWELVE

THE KEYS BENEATH THE ICE

It had been weeks since Orakai slept normally.

Sleep had become a flickering slideshow of maps, ancient carvings, and questions no one dared to ask.

One morning, while lighting her cigarette and sipping coffee, she muttered to herself:

"It's not that we didn't know. It's that we stopped looking."

The Clue is in Plain Sight

She stared at a satellite image of South America.

Somewhere near Lake Titicaca, where the air was thin, and the stones were impossibly shaped. Puma Punku. No mortar. No explanation. And angles perfect to the decimal.

Why and How would a civilization with no written language carve stone like modern engineers?

That same week, her research led her to a blog about Eastern Turkey.

A stone tablet unearthed near Mount Ararat—a region tied to myth and history.

Carvings that looked eerily like a double helix.

Yes, the same one that they showed in the series "Manifest"

"They weren't primitive," she whispered.

"They were silenced."

Her deeper dives revealed that many ancient sites across the world—India, Egypt, Peru—were under strict surveillance and restricted access.

Protected under the banner of "preservation," yet many of them had never been thoroughly studied or documented. Something didn't add up.

She stumbled across whistleblower notes from ex-archaeologists, hinting that certain global heritage councils, with enormous funding, weren't just preserving the past—

They were curating it.

"Who decides what gets seen... and what gets buried?" she wondered.

A Message is Etched in Earth

Everything began to look connected.

Stone structures weren't just ceremonial—they were data.

Archives carved to withstand storms, wars, even time.

The same geometries repeated across continents.

The same orientation to stars.

The same magnetic alignments.

"They didn't forget.

We were made to forget."

A few nights later, a message arrived.

"Some questions aren't meant to be asked."

There was no sender.

No trace.

Orakai paused.

The fear wasn't in what they might do to her—

It was in the realization that someone was watching.

And that meant one thing:
She was getting close.
The Journey Begins
That night, she booked a one-way ticket to Ushuaia.
A City in Argentina, the southernmost city in the world.
Not to run away, but to run toward something.
Not the past.
Not a theory.
But a hidden structure beneath the myths of time.
The genesis wasn't a story.
It was a network.
And someone had been rewriting its code.

CHAPTER THIRTEEN

GATEWAYS IN DUST

The airplane hummed with the quiet of a long-haul flight.

Orakai stared out the window, watching the clouds shift like thoughts she couldn't quiet.

The seat beside her remained empty—until final boarding.

A tall woman in a muted trench coat slid in with effortless grace.

She nodded, opened a thick book filled with diagrams, and didn't speak for a while.

Her name was Slizer.

That wasn't her real name, she said.

Just the one she used when she didn't want to be followed.

Turbulence shook the plane, but Slizer barely flinched.

"Funny," she said with a dry smile, "we fear things we can't control. But the real danger is always hidden in plain sight."

Orakai looked over.

That's how it began.

Their conversation unraveled like a thread they'd both been pulling their entire lives.

Both had walked away from systems designed to silence.

Both were chasing questions that weren't safe to ask.

"Truth is a responsibility," Slizer said. "Most people avoid it to stay comfortable."

Orakai just nodded. She'd lived through that truth.

They landed. Same guesthouse. Same booking.

Coincidence? Maybe. But it didn't feel like one.

That evening, under a flickering lantern on a stone bench, Slizer opened a leather folder—real documents, not digital. Old photographs. Flight logs. Declassified memos.

"This is from Operation Highjump—1947," she said. "Officially a U.S. research mission. Unofficially... they found something."

Coordinates blacked out in ink.

Satellite images that didn't match any current mapping.

Thermal signatures—too symmetrical, too warm to be natural.

"There are entire zones beyond the ice shelf scrubbed from public maps," she said.

They flew again. South. Then farther to a research Center in Ushuaia.

The plane touched down on the edge of the ice shelf, the runway etched into whiteness like a scar.

The cold hit like a punch.

And the silence—it wasn't peace. It was observation.

"This place is monitored," Slizer said as they crossed the ice in a snowmobile.

"My contact—used to be military—said he saw something here in '99. Mapping mission. A wall. Black. Smooth. Warm."

"Warm?" Orakai asked, blinking.

Slizer nodded. "Not natural. And now it's gone."

The science station loomed ahead, sterile and silent. But Orakai could feel it.

They weren't alone here.

Inside the station, whispers and glances followed them. Doors were locked that didn't need to be. Questions answered with shrugs.

But beneath their feet, something ancient stirred.

Orakai traced the patterns on Slizer's maps.

Thermal anomalies shaped like geometry.

Symbols matching proto-Sumerian glyphs found across continents.

"There were legends," Slizer said, "of civilizations that vanished, leaving behind gates locked in ice. We weren't meant to open them."

"Maybe this whole world is a cover," Orakai whispered, eyes unfocused.

"And what's beyond is the author's note we were never meant to read."

They didn't make promises

.

They didn't need drama or declarations.

Just two women—awake, aware, and no longer alone.

Whatever was buried beneath Antarctica's silence, they would face it together.

Not for glory. Not for fame.

But because once you see the truth, you can't pretend it was never there.

And somewhere beneath the ice— the door was waiting.

CHAPTER FOURTEEN

Eyes That Watch

Two days after arriving in Ushuaia—the last major city before Antarctica—Orakai and Slizer felt a shift. The air was different.

Every local they spoke to had the same tight smile and vague answers. "No one goes past the zone," they'd say. No explanations.

Slizer had arranged to meet Emil, a former map technician who once worked with satellite imaging. He came alone, hood up, sunglasses on despite the cloudy sky.

"They're lying," Emil said simply. "The maps you see? Fake. The data? Edited. What's out there... it's not ice. Not all of it."

He passed them a weathered hard drive, old and dented. Inside were thermal images, GPS anomalies, and a folder titled WALL and took a leave.

It showed something stretching across parts of Antarctica—a massive boundary, straight and unnatural. No natural formation is that perfect. Satellite images had been altered.

Time-stamped pictures had been swapped out.

Then, that night, Orakai's phone glitched. Her encrypted folders were accessed. Slizer's device went blank for hours.

In the morning, Orakai noticed a man in a grey coat near the docks.

She saw him again near the café. And again that night, in the bookstore. Same man. Same coat. Always just… watching.

"They're on to us," Slizer said. "This happens to people who look too deep."

They cut off their phones, switched to paper, and even whispered in public. Everything felt monitored. But the questions kept multiplying.

That night, on the rooftop of their inn, with the Southern Ocean stretching dark and endless before them, Orakai asked the one question she feared most.

"What if there's something beyond the ice? What if… we're not allowed to know?"

Slizer didn't respond. Instead, she pulled a sealed envelope from her jacket

"This came anonymously. Months ago. I didn't take it seriously until now."

The letter inside was short:

"The gate is not where they told you. **72° 0′ S, 100° 0′ E.** There is a wall. Beneath it lies the truth. You're already late."

Orakai's heart dropped. A wall? Beneath it?

At that moment, her phone—still off—vibrated once. A single offline message from

Miko, somehow pushed through:

"I found something. You need to hear this. It's about the wall."

The same wall.

She looked up at Slizer, who was now staring at her with narrowed eyes.

"What if that wall... is hiding another world?" Slizer whispered.

Silence followed.

They were no longer chasing questions.

Now, the questions were chasing them.

CHAPTER FIFTEEN

BENEATH THE SNOW

Orakai stared at the coordinates on her notebook as though they'd blink and change.

72° South, 100° East.

She'd seen them too many times now. It wasn't just a random point—it was a pattern.

Earlier that evening, Slizer had dragged her into a small café tucked behind the back alleys of Reykjavik's research quarter.

It was there they met Aries, a tall dark man known for bending rules quietly. He worked in the logistics and expedition supply circuit—legal on the surface, but with enough backdoors to let truth slip through.

He looked around cautiously, leaned forward, and dropped a black-and-white printed satellite image on the table.

"This image was never meant to leave the vault," he whispered. "Taken by a decommissioned weather satellite. The original was scrubbed. But I pulled a cached copy from a system backup no one thought still existed."

Orakai squinted at it.

Beneath the white blur of ice fields, a distinct circular structure showed through the thinner glacial sheet—faint, symmetrical. Mechanical-looking.

"Is this at the coordinates?" Slizer asked.

Aries nodded once. "Exactly. And whatever that is, it's ancient. The ice layers over that region suggest it's been buried for tens of thousands of years. Long before humans ever built anything remotely complex."

Orakai looked at Slizer. "You told me your sketches... they were based on signals?"

Slizer reached into her bag, pulling out pages filled with drawings—half geometry, half intuition. "We picked up electromagnetic pulses. Rhythmic, like language. Not radio. Not natural. I started dreaming them before I understood what they were. Then they started showing up in research sensors across multiple expeditions."

"Did you report them?" Orakai asked.

Slizer smirked. "We did. But after that, we got pulled from the mission. Quietly. Our gear was confiscated. Our recordings deleted."

Aries added, "That's when I started looking deeper. Do you know what the UN refers to that sector as in its sealed documents?"

He pulled another paper: **PROJECT BOUNDARY.**

"Not a name you'll find online. It's a classified perimeter, built after the Cold War. A 'buffer zone' they claimed was to monitor glacial stability."

Slizer scoffed. "Yeah, because ice needs armed guards and blacksite tracking beacons."

Orakai leaned back, stunned. "So this was never about ice. They're hiding something. But what is it?"

Aries hesitated. Then: "There's a theory among some of us... that beneath the Antarctic shelf is a construct left behind.

Not by aliens—let's not get cinematic—but by a civilization that predated the ones we know. Maybe even Homo sapiens."

"A second genesis?" Slizer asked.

Aries shrugged. "Call it what you want. Some think it's a vault. Some, a prison. And some say it's a map to where we came from."

Silence followed. Only the soft hiss of the coffee machine kept the moment from freezing.

Then Orakai's phone buzzed.

A voice message from Miko.

She played it.

"Sis, it's not just you. I've been digging too. Old government archives—scanned PDFs from the 50s. They found something at the same coordinates. They didn't build the wall to protect people from it.

They built it to keep people from finding it. You need to go. And you need to be careful."

Her hand shook slightly. Slizer reached out and squeezed her wrist.

That night, they arranged for the expedition.

Aries said: "No phones. No trackers. No live comms."

Twelve hours later, the Recon Runner moved across an endless white void. Orakai stared through the frosted glass, watching for nothing—and yet expecting everything.

Aries finally spoke. "If you see birds, turn around. Birds don't belong out here. Last time I saw birds, we lost two men."

"What happened to them?" Slizer asked.

"They walked toward the black line in the snow and never came back. Compass stopped. Radios fried. Then a sound—low, constant, like it came from inside your own skull."

Orakai didn't reply. Her mind was already there.

Just before they reached the coordinates, the GPS blinked out. Then the crawler's lights dimmed. Static filled the comms.

Outside the foggy windshield, a perfectly vertical black line emerged on the horizon.

Orakai stepped out first.

Her boots crunched on untouched snow. The cold was sharp but quiet. She walked toward the wall—no visible end, no beginning. A presence, more than a structure.

It wasn't made of stone or ice. It looked like compressed darkness. Dense. Solid. Deliberate.

Then she saw it—symbols. Not letters. Equations. Like someone had carved math into the side of a god.

Behind her, Slizer gasped.

Orakai reached out and placed her hand on it.

It hummed—a vibration not felt by the body but by the memory.

And then... something shifted. A part of the wall slid open just slightly, revealing a seam of blinding white light—not cold, not hot. Just... pure.

A voice, mechanical but almost familiar, buzzed from her comms:

"You are not authorized to remember. But you already do."

Orakai stumbled back, eyes wide.

Slizer caught her.

The wall sealed again.

Above them, a drone appeared.

Unmarked.

Silent.

Just watching.

Its lenses, like insect eyes, shimmered with shifting hues—red to violet, back again.

Orakai's breath caught in her throat.

She could feel it scanning them. Not just their faces.

Something deeper. Their choices. Their thoughts. Their Souls.

Beside her, Slizer went still.

Then the drone blinked out of existence.

No warning. No sound.

Just Gone.

That's when the forest began to wake.

A deep vibration rolled beneath the snow, not heard but felt—like the wall's pulse had followed them out. The trees trembled though there was no wind.

From deep within the timberline came a sound—a mechanical shriek, long and splitting. Not natural. Not familiar.

Slizer didn't wait. "Move! Now!"

They ran.

Boots hammering through crusted snow, dodging low-hanging limbs as they pounded down the slope.

Ice cracked beneath their feet in jagged splinters.

Behind them, something darted through the trees—fast, metallic, and wrong. Red lights flickered in the dark like a heartbeat chasing them.

"There!" Slizer shouted.

At the base of the ridge, half-buried in frost and brush, was the car—a matte-black Recon Runner. Its engine was already humming low, warm. The headlights were off, but the driver's door clicked open as they approached.

Aries sat behind the wheel, calm as a glacier, cigarette smoldering between his lips.

"About damn time," he muttered.

They dove into the back just as a shadow swept overhead.

"Drive!" Orakai yelled.

He didn't need to be told twice. The Runner tore away from the clearing, tires spitting snow as it sped down the half-frozen logging road.

Branches scraped the sides. Slizer glanced back—one final look.

The drone was there again, hovering at the edge of the trees.

Watching.

But it didn't follow.

Inside the car, Slizer finally exhaled. "That wasn't a surveillance unit. That thing was... sentient. It was waiting for something."

Aries glanced in the rearview mirror. "Yeah. I was Waiting to see if you'd come back different."

Neither of them responded.

The Runner's wheels carved a path through the frostbitten forest, headlights dimmed to avoid detection.

Shadows raced alongside them, but nothing followed. Not yet.

Orakai leaned forward, her voice low. "I touched it."

Slizer turned to her, still catching her breath. "The wall?"

She nodded. "It wasn't just reacting. It recognized me. And when it opened..."

She hesitated.

Slizer's eyes narrowed. "What was inside?"

"Light," Orakai said quietly. "But not just that. Memory. Like it showed me something I didn't see with my eyes—but felt with something older."

Aries grunted. "The kind of thing you don't come back from."

"No," Orakai said, shaking her head. "The kind of thing you don't realize you already left."

Slizer leaned her head back against the seat. Her breath fogged the window.

"And that message," she said. "On your comms. What did it mean?"

Orakai hesitated. Then, flatly: "You are not authorized to remember. But you already do."

Orakai shook her head slowly.

"Because I'm not supposed to exist?"

For a while, no one spoke.

The Runner sped through the woods, dodging old service pylons and collapsed terrain, until finally the trees began to thin.

A ripple shimmered in the air ahead—a cloaking field stretched between two ridgelines.

A moment later, the distorted silhouette of a Camp came into view. Metallic walls coated in camouflage mesh. Antennas shaped like dead trees.

A holographic sky looped above, cracked and flickering.

Aries keyed a sequence into the console. The perimeter shimmered, then parted like fog.

As the Runner passed through, the temperature shifted. Warmer. Artificial. Safe, for now.

Inside the gates, ground crews watched silently as the car rolled in.

No questions. No salutes. Just wary eyes.

They parked. Orakai stepped out, boots landing hard on the grated metal floor. She turned back toward the trees—now distant, shadowed. Far beyond them, like a heartbeat beneath the earth, the Wall pulsed once. Then went still.

Slizer came up beside her. "It's not over."

Orakai didn't look away. **"It never was."**

CHAPTER SIXTEEN

THE SEAM IN REALITY

Back at the camp, Orakai sat wide-eyed in the dark, unable to sleep.

The faint hum of the portable heater bathed the tent in a soft amber glow, but it did little to warm the unease inside her.

The words kept playing in her mind, looping like an encrypted message.

"You are not authorized to remember. But you already do."

She sat upright, heart racing. Who decided who was authorized to remember?

And why did those words feel less like a warning and more like a truth she had known all along?

Across from her, Slizer sat cross-legged, sketchbook resting on her lap, pencil moving in rhythmic strokes. Her eyes were fixed, focused, drawn to some inner vision. Without looking up, she spoke.

"I saw the symbols too," she said quietly. "They're not random. They're sequences. Like keys."

Orakai rubbed her hands together, not from the cold but from the leftover tingle that hadn't left since she touched the wall.

"But keys to what?" she asked.

Slizer finally looked up, her expression intense. "Not a place. Not a door. It's us. The keys are for something inside. The mind. Memory. Something buried."

A long exhale escaped Orakai. She glanced at her palm again. It still felt alive, like the wall had left a print under the skin. The hum from earlier wasn't just sound. It was deeper—like it reverberated through her cells.

Then Aries stepped inside the cabin. Snow still clung to his jacket and eyebrows. His breath came out in sharp, frosty puffs.

"We need to move," he said, voice low.

Orakai stood. "What happened?"

"We're not alone," he replied. "I spotted two black transports about five miles out. No national insignia. No transponders. They're cloaked."

Slizer rose immediately, her sketchbook forgotten. "Think they saw us?"

Aries nodded. "They saw us. That drone earlier wasn't just surveying. It was scanning. They know we're here."

Orakai remained still. Her eyes drifted toward the tent's flap, to the snowy horizon.

"What if we don't leave?" she said.

Slizer and Aries looked at her like she'd spoken a forbidden thought.

She stepped forward. "What if we're meant to be here? What if the wall opened because we were supposed to see it?"

Aries crouched beside her, the soldier in him at odds with the explorer.

"Maybe you're right," he said. "But we also need to understand what that means. If what we saw wasn't meant for the world to know, then we've already crossed a line no one comes back from."

All of them fell into silence.

Then her satellite phone buzzed.

Orakai snatched it up. One message. From Miko.

Her voice trembled as she read:

"It's all connected.

The wall, the disappearances, even the old maps.

I found records from 1938. German expeditions to Antarctica.

They marked similar sites in coded journals.

They spoke of a doorway. A seam in reality. They believed it led to the origin of human consciousness."

Orakai looked up, eyes wide. "The origin... of consciousness."

Aries's face paled. "That's not legend. People have died chasing that. Whole teams disappeared."

Slizer clicked her pen shut. "Then maybe we stop running. Maybe we go deeper."

They agreed to stay until dawn, just enough time to pack and disappear before the transports advanced.

But something pulled Orakai back.

Before sunrise, she slipped away and returned to the wall.

Snowflakes kissed her cheeks, but the cold no longer mattered.

She placed her palm against the ancient surface and whispered, almost involuntarily:

"If I'm not authorized... then let me remember anyway."

And for a moment, she did.

A flash of something.

A dystopian city—massive, crystalline, precise. Unlike any civilization recorded in history. It stood not in the past but beyond time.

Towering structures hummed with invisible energy.

Its inhabitants were silent, serene. Not gods. Not aliens. Just... us. Before the world began recording itself. Before the first word was spoken. Before the veil was drawn.

Then it was gone.

The wall remained unchanged. Silent. Still.

But Orakai knew something had shifted.

When she returned, the others were ready. Aries drove, Slizer watched the horizon, but Orakai sat in the back, scribbling in her notebook like her life depended on it.

As the sun rose behind them, casting golden light on the endless white, Orakai didn't look back.

She knew now:

The wall wasn't the final clue.

It was the beginning of memory.

CHAPTER SEVENTEEN

THE FIREWALL OF TRUTH

Orakai sat silently in a dim-lit room within a modest hostel in Puerto Natales, Chile—a small town near the Antarctic gateway.

They had crossed back over using a chartered vessel arranged by Aries, narrowly escaping detection by patrolling forces near the perimeter zone.

The air outside still carried the sting of the southern winds, but inside, everything was heating up.

Around her sat Aries, Slizer, and now—virtually—Miko, who had called in through a Burner phone using encrypted messaging. The signal cracked slightly, but Miko's voice was calm and calculated.

"Orakai," she said, "there's something you all need to hear.

I've been digging into a series of encrypted archives that I found through an old university server...and I came across a term repeatedly — Project Boundary."

Orakai blinked. "I've seen that phrase too. On Aries's documents. What does it mean?"

Miko exhaled, "It's what you think it is. It's real.

It's a multi-national operation that dates back to the 1950s. After WWII, when Nazi scientists were absorbed into the U.S. under Operation Paperclip, there were discoveries made... things they couldn't explain.

Not just tech, but knowledge. Ancient knowledge."

Aries leaned forward. "They found out that the Earth wasn't entirely what we were told. Beyond Antarctica, beyond what we know—there were structures, remains... possibly even entrances. But instead of telling the world, they created this project to contain it."

Slizer added:

"This aligns with what I found.

Hidden beneath the Antarctic Treaty are classified sub-clauses signed only by top-level insiders. It allows covert military activity and bans independent exploration beyond certain longitudinal points."

Miko continued, "But here's the twist. This secrecy?

It's not just governmental.

The Freemasons—ancient secret societies—are intertwined with this entire cover-up. They were never just about rituals or temples.

She continued: They've guarded forbidden knowledge about human origins for centuries.

Their symbols, like the compass and square, don't just mean balance—they represent architects of worlds. Keepers of blueprints."

Orakai's mind spun. "So you're telling me... these ancient orders were hiding scientific truths? Evolutionary leaps?

Perhaps even alien intelligence?"

Aries nodded. "They were suppressing access to what lies beneath the known Earth. Some say deep underground, others beyond the ice wall—depends on who you ask.

But all signs point to the same truth: our civilization is being deliberately kept in the dark."

Slizer pulled out a torn page from a 1920s Freemason journal she had found in Chile.

On it was a sketch of concentric Earth layers, with an inscription in Latin: "Veritas sub glacie est" — The truth lies beneath the ice.

Orakai was shaking now—not in fear, but awe. "And what about the UFO sightings? The unexplained signals?"

Miko replied, "Many aren't from 'up there.' They're from underneath. Underground or under-ice crafts, tech older than any nation-state.

Think of the 2004 Nimitz incident—what if it was a test? What if these objects aren't alien... but ancestral?"

Silence fell.

Then Aries whispered, "The final firewall isn't tech. It's belief. If we believe we already know everything, we'll never question what lies beyond."

Orakai looked out the window. "And this... This is just the beginning."

Miko's voice crackled again, "Be careful. If you're hearing all this, they probably already know you're close."

Suddenly, Slizer's device blinked. A message, from an unknown sender:

'They know you know. Turn back now.'

They all stared at each other, knowing there was no turning back.

CHAPTER EIGHTEEN

THE RECKONING BEGINS

The air inside the cabin was unnaturally still. Even in the heart of Antarctica, where wind ruled everything, the silence now carried weight—like the calm before something catastrophic.

The group hadn't spoken for hours. Everyone was processing something—whether it was the leak, the revelation, or the looming sense that they had just touched the surface of something far older and more significant than themselves.

Orakai stared out of the window. The white void outside no longer looked empty—it felt like a cover. A mask. A concealment.

What if we've been buried beneath stories... buried so deep we forgot what truth looked like?

Slizer walked in, holding a tablet. "Orakai... it's time."

She was led to the main room again, where Aries had connected the satellite modem, even at the risk of being traced.

On the screen was the decrypted video file they had discovered just days ago—one never meant for public eyes.

The video opened with blurred satellite footage, slowly sharpening into an unmistakable structure beneath the Antarctic ice. It was ancient, impossibly symmetrical. A dome.

No—a facility. There were etchings on the wall. Symbols never seen in public academia.

Slizer zoomed in. "They match the carvings found in ancient Peru. In Sumer. Even in the underwater ruins near Yonaguni, Japan."

Orakai's breath caught. "What if we all came from here?"

Miko called on the backup phone.

"I've traced the uploader. Codename Ashren. Ex-member of a covert international think tank. Not just whistleblowers.

They were scientists, historians, and yes—some were high-ranking officials who left because they couldn't be complicit anymore."

"And the message?" Orakai asked.

Miko hesitated.

"It said: Genesis was the spark. The flame comes next. The world you know was written. But the truth is older than ink."

Aries turned his laptop.

"There's more." He pulled up ancient texts, declassified archives, and forbidden documents: Fossilized microbes found in Martian meteorites.

Ocean floor samples revealing non-earthly isotopes.

Genomic studies showing non-human DNA fragments in parts of the population. Not mutations—insertions.

"What if LUCA wasn't just a universal ancestor," Emil said, "but a programmed origin?"

Slizer added, "You know how every bird, plant, reptile, and even fungi share strands of genetic code? That's not random. That's a framework."

Orakai whispered, "Like a design?"

"Exactly," Slizer said. "Life didn't just happen. It was allowed to happen. At a very specific moment. With boundaries we're only beginning to question."

They went quiet again.

Orakai recalled something from her childhood—a book her teacher had once read, about the Tower of Babel.

How humanity once spoke the same language. How they were divided for seeking too much. What if that wasn't punishment? What if it was containment?

Aries slowly turned the screen again. "The name Project Boundary keeps showing up. And it's not a codeword. It's a global containment agreement... signed in 1963."

Orakai stood slowly. "Signed by who?

Aries looked at her, grim. "UN delegates. But the strings go deeper. A hidden circle.

The Freemasonic seal showed up again... only this time, tied to something called the Covenant of Silence."

"And what's behind the Boundary?" she asked.

Slizer clicked again. A freeze frame from the leak—a flicker, a shadow—barely visible.

But unmistakable.

Not a building. Not a ruin.

A door.

Built into the ice.

With something beneath it... glowing faintly.

Miko's voice returned. "They built the wall. To keep people out. Or maybe... to keep something in."

The storm outside began to rage harder, hammering against the windows.

Orakai's eyes burned with realization.

"This world—our governments, our religions, even our sciences—have been part of a screenplay. Written to limit us, not liberate us. The real origin of life isn't just ancient—it's intentional. And somewhere beyond that wall... is the answer."

A faint ping sounded on the laptop. A live message from Ashren.

Only one sentence:

"This is not a conspiracy. It is the unfinished chapter of your evolution."

Orakai looked up.

"We're not meant to stay in this cage."

She turned to the group. Her voice steady, her mind sharper than ever.

"Futurekind isn't coming. We are it. But not everyone will survive the truth."

As the snow storm raged and the power flickered, Slizer handed her a printed page—coordinates. Again.

"We go soon. If they don't stop us first.

CHAPTER NINETEEN

THE BOUNDARY UNVEILED

The coordinates Slizer handed Orakai pulsed with finality—latitude and longitude carved into paper with almost no margin for error. No one asked how he got them. No one needed to.

Within hours, the storm had eased just enough to move.

The cabin, once a sanctuary, now felt like a relic of the world they were leaving behind.

A thin veil of frost clung to the windows, and the hum of equipment had gone eerily quiet, as if even the machines were holding their breath.

They packed quickly—thermal suits, emergency rations, solar comms, encrypted drives, and three sled-mounted drones.

Aries managed to activate one of the older Russian transport vehicles—a tracked Vityaz DT-30—once used for polar research. It hadn't moved in years. But it roared now like it remembered its purpose.

The journey across the icy expanse felt surreal. Antarctica stretched infinitely white, but under this endless canvas lay the secrets they were chasing—literal layers of time and deception.

As the vehicle rolled forward, Orakai stared at the horizon.

She felt it again: the faint pressure in her chest. A pull. As if something beneath the ice was calling to her specifically.

"You feel that?" Slizer asked, unprompted, as if reading her mind.

She nodded. "It's like... gravity, but not physical."

Slizer, flipping through an old CIA PDF.

Aries had decrypted earlier, added, "It's called the Ross Displacement. Measured anomalies in local gravity fields. But they were dismissed. Buried under 'ice shift theories.'"

He paused. "Even though the readings matched ones found near the pyramids of Giza."

As they neared the coordinates, the Vityaz's radar picked up irregular topography beneath the ice sheet—perfect circles, hexagons even.

Too symmetrical to be natural. Aries overlaid the satellite data. A dome. Fifty meters tall. Covered in 4,000 years of compressed snow.

They stopped. The storm hadn't reached this far yet. Just wind and white silence.

Miko, still communicating via satellite phone from her nearby relay base, uploaded one last file.

"You'll need this," she said. "It's not just a map. It's a neural pattern overlay.

Designed by the original think tank members. Project Boundary wasn't just physical—it was psychological. You need to stay aware, or it breaks you."

Slizer looked at her image on the screen. "Define breaks."

"They said the last two who made it near the core—one vanished. The other came back with a completely different EEG pattern. He kept saying the same phrase: 'I saw before we began.'"

They reached the marked location by mid-afternoon.

The sun never set this time of year—it just circled the sky like a predator.

Slizer and Aries drilled down carefully, guided by the depth sensors. Ten meters. Fifteen. At twenty, the drill clanged against something metallic.

A resonance rang through the ice—like a chime. Not natural.

They cleared the surface with heat guns. And there it was.

A door.

Geometric.

Embedded with symbols they'd seen in Sumerian and pre-Incan sites. One of them pulsed faintly when

Orakai placed her hand on it. The snow around them seemed to react too—melting slightly, revealing an outer ring of glyphs.

Then a low vibration began. Like the planet was speaking.

The door hissed open.

Steam and pressure released like an exhale from Earth's buried lungs.

Beyond it, a spiraling ramp led down into darkness.

They entered.

Inside, the walls were smooth—some form of stone not native to this continent.

Magnetite laced with quartz and other rare earths.

Orakai felt her ears ring and her thoughts sharpen as they went deeper.

They passed murals—etched figures not quite human.

Tall, elongated skulls. Not alien in the way sci-fi had taught them. More... ancient.

Evolved. Some of the figures held orbs, others extended hands toward stars.

A few showed beings fragmenting into DNA helixes, then recombining.

Aries whispered, "It's a genetic map. A memory sequence."

Slizer ran her hand across one. "This isn't language. It's instruction."

They arrived in a circular chamber.

At its center: a suspended core. A globe-like device hovering without any visible support.

Humming with faint light. Around it were terminals—if you could call them that—non-electronic but reactive to touch.

When Orakai stepped close, the globe flickered.

It projected holographic constellations—Orion, Sirius, Pleiades.

Then zoomed in... Antarctica. A web of underground nodes revealed themselves—dozens of sealed sites, all interconnected.

Slizer activated a secondary panel, revealing something even more shocking—real-world maps.

One node beneath Lake Vostok. Another under Giza. One in the Mariana Trench.

All bearing the same phrase, translated from the ancient script:

"You were not born. You were released."

Then the room pulsed.

A voice—non-verbal but unmistakable—entered their minds.

"STATE YOUR FUNCTION."

Each of them heard it differently. In their own language. Their own tone. The room wasn't asking who they were. It was asking why they had come.

Orakai stepped forward. "To remember. To know. To awaken."

A pause.

Then light poured into the core.

The floor beneath them shifted, revealing fossilized remains—not human. Tall, bi-pedal, yet elegant. With multiple spines along the back. Not decayed. Preserved in stasis.

Slizer whispered, "This is the First Form."

The voice again.

"THE FINAL WALL IS NOT ICE. IT IS CHOICE."

Orakai's mind felt pierced—not painfully, but like a veil being lifted. Images flooded her—planets seeding life, beings traveling not by ship but through energy grids in space, knowledge passed not through books but frequencies.

She saw Earth being terraformed. Not all at once, but in stages. Genomes embedded. LUCA—not random. A designed divergence point. Humanity was just one version.

A message followed.

"YOUR KIND WAS THE only one to forget. Now you remember. The Boundary is undone."

The room powered down slowly.

Not all answers were spoken. Some had only just been planted. But the message was clear:

There is more.

Slizer handed Orakai a new sheet.

"Coordinates. Again."

She took it silently.

Miko's voice returned in her ear: "Whatever you saw—it's only part of it. They'll try to stop you. You're touching the center now. The lie can't hold much longer."

Orakai nodded.

"We're not running anymore. We're completing the story."

CHAPTER TWENTY

FINALE: GENESIS AWAKENED

The storm had not stopped. If anything, it had grown sentient. The winds no longer howled—they spoke. In pulses, in patterns. Like warnings encrypted in nature itself. Orakai, Slizer, and Aries still inside the cave.

Aries scanned the area with the analog infrared—anything digital glitched wildly in this place. "There's a heat source down there," he murmured, pointing toward the crevice. "Warmth inside ice. That should not be possible."

Slizer, unusually quiet, stared down. "Then it's already begun."

The narrow crevice opened into a descending shaft that seemed more carved than natural. The walls weren't jagged—they were smoothed, lined with patterns invisible to the naked eye, yet felt. Orakai ran her hand across one—shivers traced her spine.

This structure wasn't built... it was grown.

Aries looked back. "It's a root system. A living structure."

As they descended deeper, the temperature rose. Pressure increased. And beneath the layers of ancient ice, they finally reached it.

The boundary.

A massive archway—seamless, metal-like but matte, carved into the frozen wall. Beneath it, a depression in the floor shaped like a circle. Seven concentric rings, each etched with symbols resembling constellations.

And at its center: the Door.

It pulsed softly, as if breathing.

Slizer approached and held out the device they'd stolen from the abandoned sub-lab.

Static.

Then a deep hum.

The arch lit up.

Lines traced outward, forming a sphere of light that surrounded them all. Within it, they saw flashes—not visions, but memories. Humanity's rise. The construction of pyramids from above. The fall of civilizations wiped clean, not by war or disease—but resets. Intentional.

Orakai clutched her head. Flashes poured in:

• A being of pure light standing atop a South American mountain.

• Oceans draining to reveal structures.

• Cities built into the walls of Mars' canyons.

• And the same eye—the one from her dreams—watching her from across centuries.

A voice resonated.

"You are not the first to awaken in this cycle. The Seed remembers."

Slizer backed up. "This is it. This is what Ashren was hiding. Project Boundary wasn't just a containment—it was a lock. This is the gate."

Aries whispered, "What's behind it?"

The voice answered.

**"The Architects. The Keepers. The Designers.

They left. But not all of them stayed away. One remains.

The gate opens only once per aeon. And it opens now."**

The ring patterns began to rotate, perfectly synchronizing with vibrations under their feet. With no manual input, the door began to dissolve—not open, dissolve. As if phased out of this reality.

Behind it was darkness.

A room, or perhaps a void.

But not empty.

Floating at the center, surrounded by light and water suspended midair—was a sphere. The Orb.

It pulsed as they entered, sending out waves.

Each wave brought new knowledge:

• There were more gates—Tonga Trench, Sahara, under the Siberian Craton.

• Every human religion echoed remnants of the original signal.

• Homo sapiens was not the first intelligent species on Earth. Not even the second.

This was the third reboot.

Slizer muttered, "This... this is a map to everything. And a warning."

A second pulse knocked Aries back.

He gasped. "I saw Earth... but covered in machines. And then swallowed by light. Something came down from the sky—looked like a moon, but it wasn't."

Orakai stepped forward.

The orb turned red.

Then everything went silent.

A single phrase emerged in her mind:
"THE WATCHER HAS SEEN YOU."
She fell backward. The orb shattered.

The whole structure began to tremble. The chamber behind them started closing.

Slizer yelled, "RUN!"

They sprinted back through the ice tunnels, up the shaft, lungs burning, reality seeming to bend—walls flickering between rock and digital noise, time stuttering in frames.

When they emerged back onto the surface, the skies were wrong.

The stars had moved.

A shape loomed in the sky—silent, black, angular. Not visible to radar, not real to the naked eye—but their minds felt it.

And then it disappeared.

Like it had never been there.

As they caught their breath, Orakai turned back to the spot where the door had vanished.

Her vision blurred for a moment—and in the haze, she saw seven lights above, hovering in perfect formation. Her ears rang.

Aries said nothing, but pointed upward. "That... that's not a constellation."

The lights blinked in sequence. Then again. Faster now. A rhythm.

Orakai stared. "It's a language. It's communicating."

Slizer activated a decoding algorithm from his analog gear, drawing out pulses. What emerged made no sense.

Coordinates. Equations. Then a glyph. Not human.

Suddenly the ground beneath them quaked. A deep rumble rose—not seismic. Machinery.

Aries fell to his knees. "The signal activated something. But it's not from here."

They loaded back into the Vityaz, the wind picked up again. But this time, it wasn't just weather. Drones in the sky. Movement to the east.

Back at the outpost, they reestablished contact with Miko, still monitoring through analog lines. Her voice trembled.

"You triggered it. I don't know what you saw, but three more global observatories just went offline. A military satellite burned up over the Pacific. And Ashren...the line went blank."

Orakai said only one thing before the line cut:

"There's more than one gate."

Slizer handed Orakai a torn piece of parchment he'd taken from the lower chamber.

Symbols. Numbers.

A final coordinate.

Slizer looked up. "This one's not on Earth."

Orakai's breath caught. "Then we're not done."

The lights in the cabin blew out. Outside, the wind stopped.

In the sky, a single red dot blinked. Then two. Then seven—in perfect alignment.

And as the final flicker of light dimmed inside the cabin, *Orakai whispered:*

"Let the Age of Downfall begin."

Trailer – Futurekind : The Age Of Downfall

The world stands on the edge of truth—yet truth is what it fears the most.

After uncovering fragments of buried knowledge, Orakai, Slizer, and Aries return from Antarctica with more questions than answers. The whispers of ancient civilizations echo louder than ever.

And just when the silence threatens to bury their progress, a voice calls back—Aries, returns with secrets too dangerous to publish, too real to ignore.

What if the pyramids weren't just monuments but machines?

What if the stars above and the energy within are not myths—but mechanisms?

What if the greatest structures on Earth were not built to worship gods, but to transmit something far greater?

*Stay tuned to find that out in **"The Age of Downfall"**..*

A Message From The Author

Hey you,

If you're reading this, thank you—not just for holding this book, but for being open to something deeper.

Futurekind: Genesis was born from a space we often find ourselves in—quiet, uncertain, and searching for meaning. This isn't just a story. It's a reflection of what many of us have felt but couldn't always explain.

Orakai's journey isn't just hers. It belongs to all of us who've questioned what we were taught, who've felt like something inside us remembers more than the world admits. Those who've been broken, only to uncover a new kind of strength.

I didn't write this to impress. I wrote this to connect—with those who feel, think, and see beyond the surface. If even one line stays with you, or if something in these pages makes you pause, reflect, or feel seen—then something real has happened between us.

We are all evolving. Slowly. Quietly. Together.

Thank you for walking a part of this path with me.

Stay tuned for Volume 2 –

Futurekind: The Age of Downfall.

In resonance,

Angel Ghosh : *The Author of Futurekind.*